Klara's New World

BY JEANETTE WINTER

Alfred A. Knopf ✥ New York

THIS IS A BORZOI BOOK PUBLISHED BY ALFRED A. KNOPF, INC.

Copyright © 1992 by Jeanette Winter
All rights reserved under International and Pan-American Copyright Conventions. Published in the
United States by Alfred A. Knopf, Inc., New York, and simultaneously in Canada by Random House
of Canada Limited, Toronto. Distributed by Random House, Inc., New York.

Library of Congress Cataloging-in-Publication Data
Winter, Jeanette.   Klara's new world / by Jeanette Winter.
p.   cm.
Summary: A Swedish family faces many hardships when they immigrate to America in
search of a better life.
ISBN 0-679-80626-1 (trade) — ISBN 0-679-90626-6 (lib. bdg.)
[1. Emigration and immigration — Fiction. 2. Swedish Americans —
Fiction. 3. Family life — Fiction.] I. Title.   PZ7.S7547Am 1992   [Fic] — dc20   91-30212

Manufactured in Singapore   10 9 8 7 6 5 4 3 2 1

For my mother and father,
Signe and John Ragner

Our little plot of land was poor and full of stones. Papa struggled to clear a field for planting, but it barely produced enough food for us to live on. Now there was no rain, and the crops were dying. Mama and Papa worried that our food wouldn't last through the winter.

Our old cow stopped giving milk. We slaughtered our last pig. Mama was running out of flour to bake bread. If our luck didn't change, I knew I would be hired out to rock babies' cradles and tend geese and pigs on the big manor farm, though I was not yet eight years old.

Then one day a letter came to Papa from America:

Dear Nils, my friend in the Homeland,

Greetings from my family to you and your wife, Astrid, and to your daughter, Klara. We are happy to have left Sweden and the stones of Småland to come to America. The land is beautiful and fertile. Everything we plant grows wonderfully. We eat wheat bread and meat every day. We have as much milk, butter, and eggs as we want. And the animals are large and healthy. Everyone who works hard can live well here.

People from all the countries of the world live together and have the freedom to practice the religion they prefer.

It would please me for you to come to America, too. There is room here for all. If you come, you should sell all you have. You will need the money for the journey and to buy land. Bring with you only what you can carry and food that will not spoil at sea. I hope to see you in America.

Your far away friend,
Bertil

Every evening Papa read the letter to Mama. I heard them whispering late into the night. They talked of sailing to America to find a better life. It would mean leaving everything behind—the cottage where I was born, my aunts and uncles and cousins, even Grandfather.

At last it was decided. We would leave for America in the spring. All through the winter darkness we prepared for the journey. Mama sat at her loom weaving cloth for new clothes. Papa built our America trunk, and Grandfather decorated it. We sold our workhorse to buy food to eat on the ship. I helped Mama bake flat bread. We prepared salted herrings, and salt pork, and dried beef. We made cheese and butter, and dried many apples.

When spring came, we held an auction and sold everything we couldn't take to America: Papa's plow, the beautiful painted clock, Mama's loom, the cradle she had rocked me in, the little wagon that Grandfather had made for me. Our old cow was led away. There was so much that we would miss. But most of all we would miss Grandfather. He said he was too old to make so long a journey, and he couldn't leave Grandmother, who lay in the church graveyard.

The days before we left were spent filling knapsacks, baskets, and the America trunk. We packed Papa's heavy tools, his gun, and his fishing tackle at the bottom of the trunk. Then our kettles, pots, wooden plates, mugs, knives and forks. Then Mama's spinning wheel, needles and thread, bedding, soap, clothing, and the family Bible. We filled baskets and sacks with the dried meat, smoked herring, flat bread, cheeses, butter, flour, coffee, sugar, potatoes, dried apples, salt and pepper, and brandy for seasickness.

One morning before dawn, Uncle Magnus was at the door with his wagon to take us to the ship. We piled everything we owned into the wagon. Kinfolk came to say good-bye. I hugged Grandfather one last time. He pressed a little pouch into my hand. "These are seeds, Klara. Plant them in America," he said. "Remember Sweden."

As we rode away, we could see Grandfather waving after us until the wagon went over the first hill. I held the pouch of seeds tight in my hand. Here and there along the road neighbors stepped out to call a final good-bye. "Come see us in America," Papa called back.

We traveled all day. That evening we reached the port at Gothenberg. There were many families like ours bound for America. The ship looked much too small to hold us all. Uncle Magnus helped us carry our belongings on board. Then the captain called for everyone who wasn't sailing to America to go ashore, and we had to say good-bye to Uncle Magnus.

It was so dark and crowded below deck that we could barely see or move. This was to be our home for many weeks. There was only a rough straw mattress in our small space. The America trunk served as a table. Papa stretched a blanket between two posts and made a hammock for me to sleep in. Mama unpacked our kettles, pots, and plates. She would take her turn cooking for us at the big stove in the galley. There was great confusion as everyone set up housekeeping, yet it seemed cheerful and happy.

Early next morning we set sail. We stood on deck to catch a last glimpse of Sweden. A pastor on board gave a farewell sermon, and we prayed for a safe voyage. As the coast disappeared even Papa had a tear in his eye. I heard him whisper, "My homeland, farewell."

At sea, Mama and Papa and I spent as much time as we could on deck, bundled against the cold wind. Those who were seasick stayed below, where the air was close and sour.

On clear days the small deck was crowded. We shared food from home and told stories. I played hide-and-seek with new friends. Old Gustaf, who came from our village, played his fiddle, and we danced and sang to his music. On Sunday mornings the pastor led prayers, and Gustaf played hymns on his fiddle.

Then one day a heavy wind blew. The sea was rough. The ship rocked so wildly that we could barely walk. Cold waves rushed across the deck. We stayed below. Trunks and benches moved about as if possessed. Barrels of milk and ale rolled and knocked against each other until their contents spilled out. The sailors closed the hatch against the rain and sea. Soon we could barely breathe. No one could cook, and we had no fresh water to drink.

I became dizzy and hot with fever. Mama and Papa watched over me. I thought of Grandfather's words, "Remember Sweden."

The storm raged for two days and two nights. On the third day the sea was calm. My fever lifted, but many other passengers were still sick. The fever was spreading on the crowded ship.

A little boy, only eight months old, died during the night and was buried the next afternoon. The ship's carpenter built a tiny coffin. We sang hymns, and the captain said a prayer. Then the sailors lowered the coffin into the sea. The waves quickly covered it.

For almost two months we saw only sky and water. The fever claimed more passengers. Our food supplies were low and spoiling, but the promise of a new life kept us going. I knew I would never see Sweden again, for I heard Papa tell Mama that this was a trip you make only once. I held tight to Grandfather's gift.

Then one day a little bird flew onto the railing. It had ventured too far out to sea and just wanted to rest its weary wings. The little bird was our first messenger from land. In the next few days we saw many birds and dolphins. Mama said we must be close to America. Then someone shouted "Land!" and everyone rushed to the rail. America at last.

We sailed into a large bay filled with ships of every kind flying flags from many countries. What a grand view! Every house we saw seemed like a palace. The captain pointed out Manhattan Island ahead of us with Staten Island and Brooklyn on either side.

We lay anchored in the bay for two days before there was room for us to dock. While we waited, doctors came on board to examine passengers to make sure no one had a serious disease, like smallpox or typhus. After we landed, we were put on a steamboat and taken to a large round building at the foot of Manhattan Island called Castle Garden.

Once inside we found ourselves among hundreds of people newly arrived in America. There were Norwegians, Finns, English, Germans, Dutch, Russians, Irish, and Italians all speaking their own language, which sounded strange to me. I couldn't understand what anyone was saying.

First we had to register with the immigration authorities. A guide who spoke Swedish offered to help Papa change our Swedish money to American and buy railroad and steamboat tickets for the journey to Bertil's home in Minnesota territory.

When Papa finished his business, he went outside Castle Garden and returned with fresh bread and sweet milk he had bought from street vendors, and fruits I had only heard about but had never seen—oranges and bananas. After so long at sea with so little to eat, the American food tasted better than anything ever had.

That night we slept on a bench in Castle Garden. Next morning Mama and Papa and I said good-bye to our friends from the ship. Our paths would take us in different directions now. Only Old Gustaf the fiddler was going with us to Minnesota.

We loaded our trunk, sacks, and baskets onto a large steamboat. I watched as people dressed in fine clothes boarded the upper deck. We were crowded together on the lowest deck with other newcomers to America, all heading west. But we couldn't understand each other. I felt alone, even though there were people all around me.

The steamboat took us up the Hudson River to Albany, where we changed to a train. I soon fell asleep to the rocking of the car. When I awoke the next morning, I looked out the window and saw fat cows grazing in tall grass. Mama and Papa looked happy.

How big America is! We were still in the state of New York and a long way from Minnesota. When we reached the city of Buffalo, we left the train and boarded another steamboat to cross the Great Lakes. Papa told me their names: Erie, Huron, Superior, Ontario, and Michigan. For three days I thought I was on the ocean again! Old Gustaf played familiar songs on his fiddle for all of us on the bottom deck.

At Chicago we changed for the last time to a small steamboat, which took us up a canal to the Mississippi River. We followed the river north, deeper and deeper into the wilderness. Once I saw Indians watching us through the trees. Old Gustaf left the steamboat at Wabasha, where his son was waiting for him. We continued north until we reached Red Wing. It had been three months since I hugged Grandfather good-bye.

How would we find Bertil's house? We had only a slip of paper with his name and town on it. No one we met could speak Swedish. Finally Papa used a kind of sign language to get directions to Bertil's house, and he hired an oxcart to haul our belongings.

We walked for miles through the forest. Then, in a clearing, we saw a man chopping wood. Papa called to him. It was Bertil. He dropped his ax and ran to greet us. Bertil's wife, Anna, ran out from the cabin holding their baby. We hugged each other, and cried for joy.

The very next day Papa and Bertil set off to find a piece of land for us. It must have good soil, plentiful water, and trees. When Papa found the right spot, he returned to show Mama and me before he filed a claim. When I saw the land, I knew that Papa would never have to struggle with big stones again.

Papa and Bertil cleared a road through the forest and cut down trees for our new house. Papa and Bertil worked quickly. I helped fill in the cracks between the logs with clay. In just seven days we had a house. It was smaller than our cottage in Sweden, with only one room, and had a sod roof like our old house. Tree stumps were cut for stools. We used our trunk for a table again, and Papa made beds out of logs. Papa said that during the long winter he would build a proper table and chairs. Mama was so happy to have a home she didn't mind having to wait for real furniture. I helped her unpack our things.

Papa borrowed Bertil's ox and plowed the land. When he planted, he set aside a small plot for me to plant Grandfather's seeds. Before winter came, we harvested a good crop of wheat and potatoes and turnips that would last until spring. Best of all, Grandfather's flowers bloomed.

Then, one winter night, Papa wrote our first letter from America:

Dear and Always Remembered Father,

*We have not forgotten you far away in Sweden. We are in the best of
health and are getting along well in America. The land is as good as we
wished for. Everything grows well. We have fifty acres and a small house
and have already harvested our first crop. We fish in our lake and hunt in the
woods. The land gives us everything we need, even broomstraws, spoons, and
toys. But I miss my dear father and have not forgotten the home of my
childhood.*

With love from Nils, Astrid, and Klara

Klara sends this flower and says to tell you she remembers.

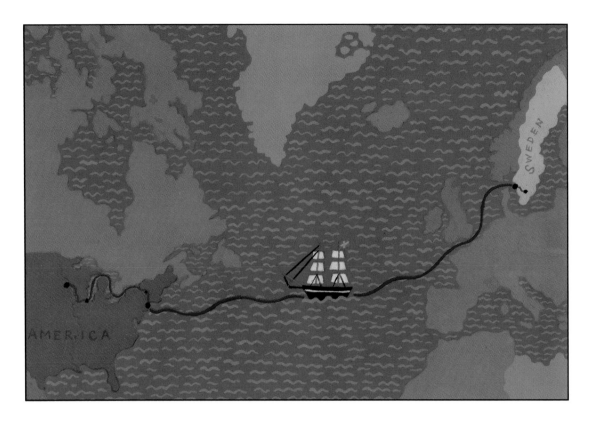

In the second half of the 1800s, thousands of Scandinavian children like Klara journeyed with their families to America in search of a better life. Sweden at the time was ruled by a king and an upper class of nobles and wealthy landowners. Klara and her family were peasants. They owned a small, rocky plot of land. The manor house where Klara would have had to work belonged to the very rich farmer who owned most of the good land in Klara's parish, or village. He was the lord of the manor, and many of the children in the parish already worked for him.

The ruling people tried to discourage the peasants from going to America. They told them that the climate was unbearably hot and that only bandits and rascals lived there. But the letters written home by the friends and relatives who had already settled in America told a different story and convinced many others to follow. Klara's journey was made sometime in the late 1860s, when crop failures and famines in Sweden compelled tens of thousands to seek a new life in America.

Klara and her family traveled to America aboard a sailing ship. This journey took six to eight weeks. If the ship was blown off course, it could take as long as three months. By the turn of the century, new and faster steamships could make the journey in days.

Castle Garden became the official landing place for immigrants in 1855. Once the immigrants had registered, they could wash up, buy food, change money, get information in many different languages, and purchase tickets for boats and railroads, as well as rest before continuing their journey.

The only way Klara's family could communicate with Grandfather was to write a letter. It was not until after the land had been cleared, the house built, and the crops harvested that Klara's family had the time to devote to this special task. This type of letter home was called an "America letter."

The flowers that grew from the seeds Klara brought from Sweden were gentians, a beautiful blue flower that still blooms in gardens and in the wild across the Midwest.

Jeanette Winter was born in Chicago, the daughter of Swedish immigrant parents. She now lives in rural Maine with her husband and is the mother of two grown sons. Among Ms. Winter's books are *Follow the Drinking Gourd* and *Diego*, a collaboration with her son Jonah and a *New York Times* Best Illustrated Book of 1991. *The Changeling*, a Swedish folk tale by Selma Lagerlöf, is her most recent book.